ONE TERRIFIC THANKSGIVING

Marjorie Weinman Sharmat

illustrated by **Lilian Obligado**

Holiday House / New York

Library of Congress Cataloging in Publication Data

Sharmat, Marjorie Weinman.
One terrific Thanksgiving.

Summary: Irving Morris Bear who loves to eat learns
an important lesson about Thanksgiving from his friends.
1. Children's stories, American.   [1. Thanksgiving Day
—Fiction.   2. Bears—Fiction.   3. Friendship—Fiction]
I. Obligado, Lilian, ill.   II. Title.
PZ7.S5299On   1985   [E]   85-726
ISBN 0-8234-0569-9

*for all the terrific Thanksgivings
at 133 Dartmouth Street*

Irving Morris Bear was perhaps the world's biggest eater. "There might be somebody else who loves food as much as I do," he thought, "but I don't know who."

Irving kept his food in seventeen cupboards and eight refrigerators in his apartment in the city.

Irving's friend Sabra Bear lived in the apartment above him. Below him lived his friend Thurp Bear. Next door to Irving lived his friend Renata Jean Bear. "I'm well supplied with food and friends," thought Irving. "What a wonderful life."

Irving's favorite holiday was Thanksgiving. "Food!" he said. "That's what makes Thanksgiving special." A few days before Thanksgiving Irving wrote down his shopping list on forty pieces of paper. Then he got on his bicycle and rode to the grocery store.

He bought lots of Thanksgiving food. His favorites were cranberry sauce, honey cakes, and marshmallows. "The sweetest parts of the meal," he said.

When Irving got home he examined all of his groceries. "Everything looks so wonderful I can't stand it! I want to eat everything right now. But it's not Thanksgiving yet. I'll have to hide my favorites so I won't eat them ahead of time."

Irving put some of his food behind his oil paintings.

He put some of it
in his washing machine.

He put some of it
in his clothes dryer.

He put some of it in his suitcase.

Irving was proud of himself for five minutes. Then he asked, "How can my food be hidden when I know where it is? I need help."

Irving telephoned Renata Jean. "Please come over."
Irving telephoned Sabra. "Please come down."
Irving telephoned Thurp. "Please come up."

When Irving's friends arrived, he said, "I have bought food for my Thanksgiving Day feast. And I want to eat my favorites right now. Could you please hide them from me until Thanksgiving Day? And don't tell me where they are. Even if I get down on my paws and knees and beg."

"You can depend on us," said Renata Jean. "You can beg until you're blue in the face, but we won't buckle under."

Irving gave his honey cakes to Thurp, his cranberry sauce to Sabra, and his marshmallows to Renata Jean. They went home with armfuls and armfuls of food.

Irving went downstairs to see Thurp. "Where are my honey cakes?" he asked.

"I won't tell you," said Thurp.

Irving bent down and rolled up Thurp's rug. "They aren't under here," he said.

Irving stared at Thurp's plants. "My honey cakes are buried in the dirt, aren't they?" he said.

Irving started to dig.

"They're not here," he said. "Why aren't they here? Please may I have my honey cakes back?"

"No," said Thurp. "I am now the official guardian of your honey cakes."

"Then I'll go up to Sabra's and get my cranberry sauce back," said Irving.

Irving went to Sabra's apartment. "I want my cans of cranberry sauce immediately," he said.

"You can't have them," said Sabra. "I did my duty. I hid them."

Irving looked in Sabra's broom closet and in her bathtub. "Only brooms and bath water," he said. "You have no imagination."

Irving grabbed Sabra's laundry bag. "I don't give up easily," he said as he dumped Sabra's dirty laundry all over the floor. "No food hidden in here. I was right. No imagination."

Irving went to Renata Jean's. "I know you hid my marshmallows and won't give them back," he said as he took apart Renata Jean's telephone and TV set.

"They're not in your telephone or TV set," Irving said finally.

"I won't tell you where I hid them even if you take apart my entire apartment," said Renata Jean.

"What a good idea!" said Irving as he overturned a sofa and looked under it. "I'm a desperate bear."

"I understand," said Renata Jean as she watched Irving pull down her drapes.

At last Irving went back to his apartment. "Some friends I have," he thought.

The next morning when Irving stepped out to get his newspaper, he found mountains of food outside his door.

"My marshmallows! My honey cakes! My cranberry sauce! Everything's back."

But there was a note with the food. It said: IS FOOD ALL YOU THINK ABOUT WHEN YOU THINK ABOUT THANKS-GIVING? LOVE, THURP, SABRA, RENATA JEAN

Irving dragged and pushed his food into his apartment. He stared at the note. "What do they mean?" he asked himself.

Irving went to Thurp's apartment. "I don't understand your note," he said.

"Think about a Thanksgiving with *only* food," said Thurp.

Irving shrugged. Then he went to Sabra's apartment. "I don't understand your note," he said.

"Think about a Thanksgiving with *only* food," said Sabra.

"That's what Thurp said," said Irving. And he went to Renata Jean's apartment.

When she answered the door, Irving said, " 'Think about a Thanksgiving with *only* food.' That's what you're going to tell me, isn't it?"

"Good guess," said Renata Jean.

Irving went back to his apartment. He kept thinking about what his friends had said.

"My friends!" he thought. "I was so busy thinking about food that I didn't think about my friends."

Irving looked at his food. "I want to share this food with my friends. I don't want to eat lonely food and this is the loneliest food I've ever seen. This is *not* what Thanksgiving is all about!"

Irving put his food away. "I have many things to be thankful for, but marshmallows, honey cakes, and cranberry sauce are not at the top of my list."

On Thanksgiving Day he telephoned Renata Jean. "Please come over."
He telephoned Sabra. "Please come down."
He telephoned Thurp. "Please come up."
Irving's friends arrived quickly.

"I'm thankful for all of you," he said, and he hugged them.

"We're thankful for you, too, Irving," said Thurp.

"Yes, even when you have food on your brain, you have goodness in your heart," said Renata Jean.

"True," said Sabra.

"I'm going to invite everyone in this building to a Thanksgiving feast," said Irving.

Twenty-four bears came to Irving's Thanksgiving dinner. "Eat, eat," he said. "Food tastes the best when you're sharing it with friends."

"This is one terrific Thanksgiving."